The Badgers of Beechen Cliff

by

Jim Edmiston

The Badger Map of Beechen Cliff

The least said about the Tunnel the better.

The Badgers of Beechen Cliff

Let me tell you a secret or two about us badgers here, shinnying up and down Beechen Cliff. Most of Somerset - badger Somerset that is - know about us. Famous, you see. There's no better place. Not for badgers. Nothing bad ever happens here. Not in my lifetime, anyway, which is about a whole year.

'You talking to yourself again, Lemmy?'

'Might be.' Just ignore him. That's Belcher. Poking his scruffy nose into other badgers' doings is what he does best.

'I said – who are you talking to?'

Don't worry, I'll get rid of him. 'A reporter from the Bath Chronic. The Great Flea Catcher of Bear Flat. Mighty Jyk the Treebender. What's it to you?'

'The Chronic? Why would you talk to them? Putting your sett on the market, are you? Got a second-hand rattletrap to sell? Ha!'

Belcher's great at pointing and scoffing. But he understands nothing. Only what he picks up in Greenway Lane the night before paper-collection day, before the rattlebang wagontraps turn up.

'That's what the human big-sizers do, Lemmy. Talk to themselves. At least, when you see *them* at it, gasping their way up the steps to the clifftop,...' He does an impersonation of a human puffing and wheezing. '... they're usually talking into one of their little boxes. They don't just talk to fresh air.'

'So, let me get this right, Belch.' That makes him

squirm. He hates being called Belch. 'What you're saying, Belch, is this – if I get myself a little box and talk into that, you'll be a lot happier. Is that what you're saying?' That's him sorted. Makes a piggy grunt. Scuffs a few leaves. That's all he can manage as he wanders off. Not one for sharpness of wit. Mind you, he's not the only pest around here. I did say there was no other place like this. But, let's face it, nowhere's perfect.

There's this magpie that keeps pestering me. At least, I think it's the same one. There's so many of them and they all have the same name – Mag. I call this one Mag 17. I count reasonably well, but I've no idea what comes after seventeen. Something pretty big, I should think, and that would amount to a entire hedgeful of magpies.

Anyway, Mag 17 seems to be following me around recently. Very jumpy. Is it because we're both black and white, I wonder? Somehow drawn to my magnetic personality? Go and chi chi a fox, I say, or one of the deer you see strolling down Lyncombe Hill as if they owned the place. But no. It's got to be me.

I can't make out half of what she's saying – all

that 'Chi, chi, chi, baja, baja, chi, chi, chi' nonsense.

'Go and bother some other black and white members of the animal kingdom. Zebras, penguins, or pandas maybe. Go on! I'd like to see you try your chi, chi, chi on some killer whale.' That would be worth seeing, wouldn't it. "Oi, Killer! Chi, chi, chi." See where that gets you.' What I do is this. I point somewhere at random and say, 'Look! Glitter, glitter. Something shiny!' And off she goes. They're bonkers, you see. Easily dazzled. Shiny things. They love them. Can't get enough of them.

I was telling you about the paradise we call Beechen Cliff. It's where we all live protected from the light and peeping big-sizers. Its tall trees, thorny bushes and thick undergrowth keep us safe. Up one side, there's Lyncombe Hill, Alexandra Park and the root vegetable feast that is known as the allotments. Along the back is Greenway Lane and the school for half-sizers. I've been told they run around there in daylight hours. Batty as well as sweaty.

Down the other side, Bear Flat, Holloway and

Bottom Edge, which eventually takes you back to the far end of Lyncombe Hill again. Complete circle. But you don't want to go wandering too far down there by mistake. It's happened, so they tell me. Oh yes. But the less said about the Tunnel the better.

The good thing about living here is the view we have of the sizers: big, half and all the other human sizes I've left out. You can see them from where I'm standing now, here, half way up the Cliff. If you look over the top of those elder bushes. There, to the north. Across the river. There they are. Not all of them, mind you. But most of them.

Piles of those lanky types in and out of those stacked-up, stone boxes they call houses. An enormous bank of orange and red lights, some twinkling and some moving up and down and from side to side.

Although there are plenty of them over here as well, planting their root vegetables for us and putting out the bins and paper every week, we try to keep out of each other's way.

It's for the best. Bear Flat is swarming with them, although, amongst all those Bear Flatters, you're unlikely to see a single bear. Not one. Believe me, I've looked. I don't get it. It's not even flat.

Gardeners and paper-stackers can go a bit backside-up now and again. If their beloved bin gets the heave-ho or a prize parsnip goes walkies. You can get an earful. The blabbering noise they make. 'Radda mocho baja baja staka ridda baja.' On and on and on. What's all that about, eh? Your idea's as good as mine.

But you don't want to meet one when they're having one of their gnashing snarlups. With their arms all flapping and their beetroot looks. Best to keep your head down and get out of their bag pile, knotted papers, thrown-away dinners and left-over snacks before they unleash the dogs.

Not that dogs bother me too much, not the bitsy ones anyway, not those behind gates. Eyes popping. Tongues dangling through the bars. But who needs it? I suppose they're all part of life's colourful what's-it. Live and let live, I say.

We do occasionally see the humans up close, as Belch mentioned, on the Cliff itself. It's not all straight up and down, you know. No. There are footpaths.

You get the half-sizers. Taking shortcuts to the park or the school. They're not so bad. They grow up to be part of the full, lanky troop of course, but while they're half-sizers, they're fairly harmless. About as much sting as a baby nettle. I was cornered by a couple of them once. They didn't go 'Radda mocho baja ridda.' They cooed like little birds and made some click click noises with their boxes.

Who else have we got? I've mentioned the magpies and the deer – they're ok – don't tangle with anybody. The mice are useless – complete waste of time. Over on the allotment, you see a few slow worms. Boy, are they fast!

But don't even waste your time on shrews.

'Morning, Brock. How are you, Brock? Blah, blah, blah-di-blah, Brock. Look at the size of this fruit fly, Brock.'

Fruit flies, for goodness sake! What is there to say about fruit flies?

Constantly rabbiting on – beg pardon - excuse the R *word*. Who's ever heard of a badger called Brock? If you come across a shrew, best to eat it right away, I say, before they start all that Brock-this, Brock-that chitchat.

We do have a leader. Yes, I must give him a big mention - he and his mate. They're getting on a bit now. Must be about twelve or thirteen. He's called... actually I can't remember what he's called. Whatever it is, nobody ever calls him it. He's just the Chief. Even his mate, Boska, calls him Chief. Even though he's old - maybe I should say ancient - he keeps us straight, keeps us out of trouble. Accumulated wisdom is what he calls it. Whatever that is.

One night, months back, after a raid on the allotments, root-veg still between my teeth, I met him and Belch and a few of the other lads coming back from Greenway Lane with a bunch of papers and finger food. And the Chief says, 'What have you got there, Lemmy?'

'Don't know,' I mumble rootfully. 'Tastes nice though. The delicate texture of potatoes, but not quite as sweet and more-ish as parsnips.'

He sniffs. 'You've not been eating them, have you? Not partaking in the guzzling sense?'

'Yeh. So?'

'Flippineck, Lemmy. That's Jerusalem artichokes you've got there. Run for it, lads! Run for it!'

I just stood and gawped at them. Then there was an almighty clap of thunder. Well, I thought it was thunder, or a tree falling over. Until I realised it was me. It blew me forward a couple of yards. All the way back home. I lay on my back all night, farting like a rhino. Next day, of course, it's all they chatted about to the girls underground. All along the twists and turns of the corridors. 'Did you hear about our Lemm? Farted like a flippin' rhino all night. Yup. More like two rhinos. I'd say three. Jerusalem artichokes. We were lucky to get out alive.'

'How do badgers learn?' the Chief shouts to everyone in earshot.

'THE HARD WAY!'

Embarrassing.

Mighty Jyk the Treebender

I know what you're thinking. Lemmy - it's a stupid name for a badger. It's barking, isn't it? I mean — Lemmy - what kind of a name is that? The thing is *they* gave it to me. No choice. When I was far too young and dangly to argue about it.

This is what happened.

One of those buzzards from Limpley Stoke down south-ish must have lost all sense of direction and found itself hovering over the Cliff. At the time, I was very small - a pudgy little nipper, they say – weeks old. I'd been eating armfuls of worms all night and should have skedaddled back underground before the sun was up. But no. Just a few more, I said to myself. So there I was digging away when there's a swoop and some crashing through the twiglets. A shower of leaves all around me.

Somebody shouts, 'Run for it, lads! Oh – sorry - and ladies!'

Suddenly, there's not another black and white snout in sight and I'm about to become buzzard breakfast. They tell me I was six feet off the ground, though I have only a vague memory of the whole affair. We hover around for a bit, the weight of my pudginess against the buzzard's determination not to let go.

'Oi!' I'm told that's what I shouted at the time. Sparkling wit. 'Oi! What are you up to, mate? Lemmy go!' He did let go, no choice, and I landed on my back leg, which is why I have this limp.

I've been called Lemmy ever since. I get teased about the limp, but I ignore them. I always keep my eyes open, however, for airborne attacks. A bit nervy, me. Especially tonight. Maybe that's why I'm jabbering on so much. But it's not the fear of buzzards that's bothering me at the moment.

I'm standing behind a beech tree. And I have to admit, when I stop to think about what happened a short while ago, my knees start shaking again. I've just seen something and I don't know what to make of it. I almost jump out of my skin when a bunch of dead leaves, yellows, browns, reds, come showering over my head. I whizz round, hackles up, nerves all a-jangle. Up on a bank, there sit Senga and Catlyn, chuckling away like a pair of idiot squirrels. Catlyn, well, she's quite nice. Senga, she's got a mouth on her.

'What's the matter, Lemmy? Seen the buzzard's ghost. Get frightened by a bad-tempered worm? Did one of those shrews pull a funny face?'

What can you do? Especially with Catlyn watching.

I don't want to let Senga away with it, but if I say anything, she'll only repeat it in her funny, squeaky, down-the-nose voice. I grunt, jiggle my fur and hobble off. Slowly. Very slowly. Taking all the time in the world, even when I hear her making some foul remark and Catlyn shushing her.

I take my time, you see, because I don't want to catch up with the grey figures who just walked past. The one stopping to bend a couple of young trees and the other, half her size, watching her carefully, before they both disappear in a swirl of mist. They were like humans with wings, but not the crash-jabbering, bin-wheeling, box-squeaking kind. Something different about them. Silent, as if they were part of the cliffside woods. The older one covered head to foot in a long, grey cloak – as I said, like wings unopened - the skin on her hands like bark. The younger one, all in black, but for the white of her face and hands.

When I get back to the sett, the Chief calls me over. 'Lemmy, come here a minute. Sit yourself down. Take the weight off your leg.'

'Yes, Chief?'

'Lemmy,...'

He scratches himself, chews something he's found in his fur, and, for a second or two, it seems as if he's forgotten what he was going to say. He looks older every time I see him. We thought he'd snuffed it a few times. 'Lemmy,' he says thoughtfully, 'you saw her, didn't you? Tonight. You saw her.'

I'm wondering if he's talking about who I think he's talking about. 'Chief? Saw who? Who did I see?'

'Come on. You know who.'

'Do I?'

He gets up, wanders round me. I watch him over my shoulder as he scratches himself again and sits down. He lowers his voice. 'Mighty Jyk the Treebender. That's who.'

I'm stunned. Because I realise that that's who it had to be. The older grey one. I knew it. I knew it when I saw her. It had to be her, the knife in her belt and the rope looped over her shoulder, just as she's described in the stories. I nod slowly.

'Yes, Chief. I think I did. I'm sure I did. Very, very old, the knife and the rope, and even more wrinkles on her face than you, Chief. Almost.'

'Thanks, Lemm.'

'It had to be her.'

'I'm sure it was.'

'How d'you know?'

'Lemmy. I'm the Chief, aren't I? I know stuff.'

'But, Chief, when you've told us stories about her, she always appears on her own and when there's big trouble brewing.'

'Hmm.' He looks around. Nobody about. With a quick sideways movement of his head, he signals to me to go inside.

This, I think, is serious. You don't just stroll into the Chief's chamber. It has to be by invitation only. And that's very rare. Not unless you want a clip round the ear. It's warm and dark inside, but for a glimpse of the full moon.

'Lemmy, is Beechen Cliff not the most peaceful, happy-pig-in-muck, badger paradise you could possibly imagine?' The moonlight catches his old silver whiskers as he speaks. 'Look out there. We have the Enemy Army of Big-sizers on all sides, but they don't really trouble us much, do they? But, of course, they could. At any time. Why is it that we're so safe here? We're happy here, we eat, sleep, mate, bring up the young ones here, and play havoc with the bins down Greenway Lane. This is worm-heaven, isn't it? It couldn't be better, could it?'

'No, Chief. Couldn't be better. Nowhere. Nowhere on Earth. Nowhere in the entire universe. Nowhere in ...em....'

'Ok, ok, don't get carried away. Let's just say that life here is good. Why is it so good?' He eyebrows me, waiting for an answer.

I think for a minute, chewing a beetle that happens to saunter by. 'Because you're our Chief.'

'Nice of you, Lemm. But that's not the reason.'

'Jyk the Treebender?'

'Yup. She keeps us safe.' That's fine, I think, but he's avoided answering my question about trouble brewing. All he's doing is nodding and muttering and moving towards the exit as a sign that I should leave now. As if the conversation is at an end. Or maybe he's already forgotten that we were having a conversation.

'So…?' I say.

'So what? Oh, yes. One other thing. Not a word to anybody, Lemmy. Ok? Keep it under your hat. There's a good lad. Have a fat night. By the way, don't go nibbling my beetles in future.'

'Right, Chief. Um, thanks, Chief,' I say at the entrance to his sett. 'One question – about the hat.'

'Just a turn of phrase, Lemm. A play on words. Don't worry about it.'

'But, Chief. If Jyk the Treebender is a sign of bad things to come, and if she's out and about now, shouldn't everybody be told. I know you don't want to start a panic. But they might panic if they see her anyway. She certainly put the wind up me. At least, there should be a committee meeting.'

The Chief scrapes at a root that's sticking out of the wall of the chamber. He walks around. Disappears down a corridor, and, after a minute or two, comes back out another one and says, 'Flippineck, Lemmy, I've just had an idea! I'll call a committee meeting.'

'Good idea, Chief.'

The Committee Meeting

Two of the committee members are Snubber, a grumpy soul, and Flora, though why she's got him for a mate is anybody's guess. A calmer badger you'll never find. She's brought her two cubs along – not committee members, of course, but they need an eye kept on them.

Though they seem to be looking after each other very well. Some sort of wrestling match by the look of it. Snubber, of course, immediately marches up to me, pokes his snout in my face, prods me in the shoulder and growls, 'What's he doing here? Since when do we let any random badger that happens by take part, casual as you like, in a meeting? He's not a committee member.'

'He is now, Snubber,' says the Chief. 'So pipe down.' The Chief's mate, Boska, has joined us. She gives Snubber one of her high and mighty looks and he backs off, shaking his head and muttering to himself.

'Never seen the like...what are things coming to... interfering riffraff... muddle, muddle, muddle... we've got rules, you know... though you wouldn't know it.'

Bogart arrives. Bogart's a big, surly badger, never says much. If he were to bang his head off a tree, the tree would come off worse. You wouldn't want to mess with him, but he's never given me any trouble. He nods to everyone. Catlyn's not here yet, but the Chief starts the proceedings anyway.

'I'll get straight to the point,' says the Chief.

'Well,' snorts Snubber sarcastically. 'Getting straight to the point, are we? That'll be a first.' His mate, Flora elbows him in the ribs and he shuts up. For now, anyway.

'I've called you here to talk about the Mighty Jyk.' He nods solemnly, appreciating the silence. 'I don't know if I told you the story of how the great-great-grandfather of my great-great-grandfather of my great…'

'Oh, for goodness sake, get on with it!' interrupts Snubber.

The Chief ignores him and continues. 'He witnessed the arrival of Jyk the Treebender. Only a half-sizer at that time. Very small, she was. Came wandering through the woods. Lost. Young half-sizers, especially that age, they've only just learnt to walk, you know. Can't find their own food or anything. Barely toilet-trained. So, when…'

'Where have you been, Catlyn?' says Boska, interrupting the Chief, who takes a deep breath and checks the colour of the sky to get some idea of the time. 'Come and sit beside Lemmy.' The Chief waits patiently and he's about to begin when she starts up again. 'That's right, dear, you sit there. I reckon some badger, who'll soon be coming up for a year old, will be choosing a mate pretty soon.' She gives a meaningful nod in my direction, and whoops and laughs like the wind swirling up a pipe. I peer sideways at Catlyn who's staring hard at the ground. 'Don't you reckon, Chief?' And she whacks him so hard on the shoulder he keels over as if he's dead.

We all watch in silence. A moment passes. Boska gives him a shake. 'Chief? Chief? You all right?'

'Poor old guy,' says Bogart gruffly.

'Oh well. This looks like it this time,' says Snubber in a very matter-of-fact way.

'Is he breathing?' asks Flora, grabbing one of her cubs by the scruff to stop the wrestling match.

'He was a good 'un,' says Bogart, lowering his head.

'We had our differences,' Snubber admits, 'but he did a good job... kind of. We'll be looking for a replacement.' He pulls himself up to his full height, which is not a lot, as if putting himself forward as a candidate.

'Well,' mumbles Boska sadly. 'I suppose the meeting's over. I'll sort out…'

'Anyway,' says the Chief, springing back into action, totally unaware that we all thought he'd died and gone to the great Cliff Hangar in the sky. 'As I was saying…'

'Might have known it,' mutters Snubber under his breath.

'When Jyk was a half-sizer, or even smaller, like one of these cubs here, she came wandering into our territory. Completely lost. Clueless. Fell down my great-great… um… great-great… um… his sett. Yup. Straight into it, newly dug, fresh golden-brown earth. You can imagine what those ancient badgers thought when they saw a pair of half-sized enemy feet poking in their faces. At first, they were terrified out of their wits. But then they realised the little thing was whimpering, bawling its head off.'

'Poor thing,' says Flora, pulling her cubs towards her.

'You're right, Flora. But look at it like this. A baby half-sizer crying loudly. What's going to happen?

The humans would have come swarming all over the cliff, that's what.'

'What happened, Chief?' asks Catlyn.

'Well, some old granny badger had the idea of feeding it. Keep its mouth full, you know. Stop it squealing. She tried a dead sparrow to begin with.'

'They're nice,' says Bogart.

'That didn't work. Oak apples, worms, shrews, snails, beetles - no good. Then eventually she tried some brambles. At last, the noise stopped. What a mess she was in with dirt and bramble juice sticking to her face like badger stripes. But a happy mess. Meanwhile, a great deal of pushing and heaving was happening underground, but the backside of the tiny wedged Jyk was refusing to move. That is, until the old granny – smart badger - and some helpers pulled down an ash sapling. Jyk took hold of it and was pulled up out of the sett as the young tree slowly straightened up.

'She didn't go flying into the air then, Chief?' says Flora.

'No.'

'A likely story,' says Snubber. 'Never seen

anything like that.'

'You can say that, Snubber,' says Boska, 'but she's helped us ever since.'

'How has she helped us? Bending trees? I've never believed in any of that mumbo jumbo.'

'She's covered our trails with leaves,' says Boska. 'Chased away snooping dogs. Left food during the hardest winters. And not that soggy bread and milk they put out for our prickly fleabag friends down Lyncombe Hill.'

'Pah!'

'She was born in these woods, Snubber,' says the Chief. 'Maybe there are no enemy houses now. But there used to be. Many years ago. Before the sky-high bangs whooped down on to the Cliff and mashed their houses into piles of rubble. The point is,' says the Chief, 'she's been in the woods again. Isn't that right, Lemmy?'

I look around at all the faces turning towards me, examining my expression. I nod.

'It's a bad sign. But before we send every other badger around here into some sort of panic, we need to find out what's going on. It's a sign for sure, but of what?' Nobody speaks, but everyone, by their silence, knows it makes sense. Then suddenly, the Chief shouts, 'Belcher! Get in here.'

'Not another one,' says Snubber, scuffing a little circle in the dirt 'Why don't we just invite all of Beechen Cliff. Have a party.'

'Show them what you found, Belcher. That paper you pulled out of a pile along Greenway.' We all surround Belcher who lays the paper down in the middle. 'We'll have to be quick. Look at the sky. It'll be daylight soon.' It's difficult to get a proper look with everyone shoving their noses in. To everyone's surprise, there is a picture of a badger.

'Well...' gasps Flora.

'A bit ugly, isn't it,' says Snubber.

'I thought it looked a bit like Lemmy,' adds Belcher, smirking. He would say that, wouldn't he. But, since I have no idea what I look like, I can't argue. Catlyn gives me a sympathetic glance.

'Doesn't matter who it looks like,' says the Chief. 'It's not a killer whale, is it? What's a picture of a badger doing in the paper? We need to find out. We need to do some detective work. Bogart. Are you up for it?'

'Sure, Chief.'

'Better take someone with you.'

Bogart grunts in agreement, stretches his neck this way and that and surveys the assembled badgers. Snubber is puffing out his chest and dancing from side to side. Belcher's stripes are shouting off his face: 'Pick me! Pick me!'

'Lemmy,' says Bogart. 'I'll take Lemmy.' Belcher lapses into a sulk.

'Good choice,' says the Chief. 'Then the less you say about the whole thing the better. I'll leave all the planning to you. Report back when you've got something.'

The first rays of the sun are hitting the treetops. Time to disappear underground until darkness returns to provide us with cover for our mission. We all go our separate ways, with Bogart and I agreeing to meet at dusk.

The two cubs roll along, nipping each other and cuffing each other round the head. As he leaves, Snubber is still grumbling to Flora about the whole meeting.   He's spouting on, saying what a load of cowpat this whole thing is about Jyk the Treebender, when there is an enormous WHOOSH and he lets out an almighty 'AAARGH!' He crashes upward through a bramble bush. And finds himself dangling upside down, attached to a rope, tied to an ash sapling. It's hard not to laugh, so I don't bother trying.   'You call this protection! Chief! Chief!'

'For goodness sake, somebody help him down.'

There's another 'AAARGH!' The sky suddenly turns black and white, there's a creak and a crash as a branch snaps.

Snubber doesn't need any help getting down.

The Mission to Greenway Lane

Have you noticed how the nights are longer now? So when we start off, it's early for us. The owls haven't even blinked yet. But we want to give ourselves as much time as possible.

There are two ways to Greenway Lane. You can go up to the top of the Cliff, sneak across Alexandra Park, saunter down through the allotments, across the field and under the wooden gate. Mind your head. The other way is much the same, but instead of heading for the sunrise end of the Lane, you turn right past the school, across the half-sizer field where they run around getting sweaty, then through a gate at the west end. Either route, you have to dodge your way through the park, and tonight, for some strange reason, every size of human seems to have gathered there. Lots of them. I reckon more than seventeen. Yep. There they are. Humans in the tripping dark! What can be going through their big, daft heads? They won't be able to see where they're going. I say to Bogart, 'I can smell wood starting to burn, but I don't smell any dogs. Do you?'

'No,' he says. 'Just hundreds of enemy and they smell bad enough. Let's go.'

We go for the eastern gate. This is Bogart's idea and it's a good one. Opposite the gate there's a corner with a whole mix-match of the kind of stone houses the humans live in. They're always throwing away stuff. Only Bogart doesn't call it *stuff*. He calls it *clues*.

The carrots smell fresh as we cross the allotments, but we agree to leave them until the return journey.

'Hello,' says Belcher, sprouting up in the middle of the dandelions and plantain.

'Keep it down,' says Bogart. 'What're you doing here?'

'Eating carrots – mmmm! Nice. Don't get sniffy. There's plenty for everybody.'

I ask him if he knows there is a clutter of humans in the park.

'So? It hasn't stopped you either, has it?' Then he suddenly twigs. 'When do you two ever go out foraging together? Unless, of course, you're ... on the mission.' We say not a peep, but that's enough for Belch. 'Let me come. Go on. I'm great at this sort of Project X thingy. Honestly. I am. I did find the badger picture after all. Which doesn't really look anything like you, Lemmy. Far too ugly... the picture, I mean. Please, Bogart. Please.' Bogart and I look at each other. Bogart sighs.

'Ok. But keep quiet.' Belcher clamps his mouth shut and nods excitedly.

Nosing our way through the long grass and

nettles at the edge of the field, we reach the gate and on the other side there's one of the humans' rattletraps. It smells hot. It's just been used. At night they have two beams of moonlight searching the road. Don't always bother to stop if they see us crossing, of course. So you have to be careful. This particular one has a dog inside. The sight of us drives it nuts. I freeze at first. I hadn't smelt it as I came across the field.

'Lemmy.' A whisper creeps out from under the rattletrap. 'Lemmy. Watch out for the dog.'

'Catlyn? Is that you? Catlyn? It's all right. The dog's trapped inside. It's safe to come out.' Two shiny eyes appear and a suspicious, little nose sniffing the air.

'Oh, thank Jyk it's you. I could hear it, but I had no idea where it was.'

'Hah!' laughs Belch. I give him a hefty nudge which quickly shuts him up.

'Since you're here, Catlyn,' says Bogart, 'we should be able to get this mission accomplished much faster. Belcher, you and me, we'll go down the hill and start there. Lemmy, Catlyn - you start with that house up there. Watch out for dogs on the loose. And I shouldn't need to tell you about rattletraps along Greenway.'

We know the dangers. But there's something strange about tonight. Very still. Dogs don't wander around on their own along this lane, but you can often smell them outside in a garden. Not tonight. They must all be inside. No sign of any pamper-tinkled cats either. There's usually one or two out and about, being careful where they put their tippy toes. It's odd and I don't like it.

As Catlyn and I cautiously inspect the first house, a fox plods by. He shakes his head, says some gibberish, but, since neither of us speaks fox, we haven't a clue what he's on about. He shrugs and goes on his way.

The boxes and buckets of rubbish look promising. Catlyn and I put our weight on the edge of one of the boxes and it tips over on to its side. Being smaller, she nuzzles her way in. Meanwhile, I start to take apart a pile of papers ready to be collected by the rattlebang wagontraps in the morning. Bogart was right about choosing tonight - the night before it all disappears.

I have a pile of papers between my teeth and I'm pulling them free from the rest, when the sky starts to burn. No kidding! It's on fire!

I run out into the road to see Bogart galloping up towards me. Some way behind him, Belcher's gormless face appears over the top of the bucket he's been investigating. As he's crawling out, the whole thing topples over with him still inside. Bogart looks over his shoulder to see bucket and screaming badger rolling round the corner down Lyncombe Hill. Always suspected he wasn't a genius.

'Come on, Lemmy. Let's get out of here.'

I start to run alongside him, but realise Catlyn isn't with us. 'Wait!' I say. 'Where's Catlyn?'

'Go fetch her,' says Bogart. 'I'll meet you at the end of Greenway. At the west gate.'

I discover Catlyn edging backwards out of the upturned box. But she can hardly move. She's got herself entangled in some netting. She looks like she's been shoved into a string bag. I immediately start to gnaw away at the fibres. All the while, the flashes of fire and lightning are going on overhead. My natural instinct is to get out of here. Fast. The explosions are ear-shattering. I tug and bite at the strings. 'Can you move now?' It's getting easier. Her back feet are not trapped now. I tug at a few more. There's a crash overhead, the sky lights up and a gigantic dandelion of silver light spreads everywhere.

We hobble our way along Greenway Lane – Catlyn still hampered by the net ensnaring her, and, me, well, I hobble at the best of times. We pass a few mice, a weasel and a deer in a panic, wondering which direction to run in.

'What's going on?' I ask Bogart when we see him. 'Is it what the Chief was talking about? The sky-high bangs that broke up the stone houses?'

'No. You two aren't old enough to have seen this before. It happens every year. They start a big fire in the park and then the sky goes wild with their spinning moons and shooting stars and flames. The noise is terrible. It's always terrible. Come on. I know another way through their gardens.'

'What about Belcher?' asks Catlyn. 'Where is

he?' Bogart shrugs and we follow him across the sweaty field, past the school and under a fence into the gardens. Here, we're surrounded by baffling scents – dandelions, compost, sheds, birdseed, hedgehogs' bottoms - so we're glad to have Bogart's experience with us.

There's no sign of anyone. One or two lights are on, but maybe everyone is in the park. The noise goes on and on. The smells of fire and clothes and burning meat and roasting parsnips and human sweat and boots and recently used rattletraps are everywhere. It's repulsive, but we're used to it. It keeps us out of harm's way – most of the time.

We crawl up a bank, along part of a wide stone wall and drop down into another garden.

'Stop here,' says Bogart, his chunky paw barring our way. He knows something. From nowhere, it seems, out of the blackness, a monstrous, black dog rises up from the moon-shadow of the house. It roars and spits and claws at the air. But, incredibly, Bogart says, 'Don't worry. Watch this. Stay behind me. Let me handle this.' I'm looking for an escape route but there's no time for that, even if there is one. So I cower behind

Bogart while Catlyn cowers behind me.

Another sparkling starburst crashes around us and lights up the foul creature. Did I already say it was big? There's a lurch. A vibration in the ground that tingles up through my feet and makes my ribcage quake. And it launches itself towards us. My heart is racing like it's about to leg it without me. But Bogart doesn't seem the slightest bit bothered as it thunders straight for us, its muzzle wet with saliva and menace. Then, for no reason that I can see, it stops in mid-air. It's inches from wrapping its teeth round Bogart and it stops. A sudden eek-worthy stop. Then I see why. It's tied by a long rope to the wall of the house.

Bogart turns to us, smiling and nodding. He does a little bow. The dog snarls, shakes its stupid, ugly head, stinkingly close, but it can't do a thing. Not a thing. I almost feel sorry for it, but dogs are so dumb. They'll do anything even the smallest-sizers tell them. So I pee on its grass, wrinkle my nose at it and we move on to the next garden.

It has its own hazard. Seems to surprise Bogart as well. We move and a light goes on. We stop for a while and it goes off. But when we head for the other fence again, it goes on again. When we stop in our tracks, expecting someone to appear, the light goes off. No one comes. I notice a hedgehog eating something at the door. Some slop by the smell of it.

We need to do some excavating under the fence to get through to the next garden. There is a light in this house. Inside, there is a human shape staring out. I should be afraid, but... .

'Lemmy,' says Catlyn, 'what are you doing? Are you mad? Let's get out of here.' But I don't move. I can't move. I see the face. I've seen its ancient lines before.

'It's Jyk,' I whisper. 'It's her.' Catlyn goes into some sort of faint. Rolls over onto her back. Bogart is snuffling around wondering what to do, searching for another way out. But I just stand there. Standing beside Jyk is a half-sizer. To me, they look alike. Only, many years separate them – more than seventeen I should think. This one, the half-sizer, moves away from the light, steps outside and still I don't move. She walks past me and looks at Catlyn. Then I see that Catlyn hasn't fainted. The netting that is still wrapped round her shoulders and front legs is caught on a piece of wood sticking out of the ground. As this daughter of Jyk bends over her, avoiding her sharp teeth and claws, she cuts away the string and sets her free. Bogart and Catlyn make a dash for it, while I just sit and watch mesmerised till she moves back inside.

By the time we get back to the Cliff, the thuds and screams, the showers of fire and flying beams of light are beginning to die away. Amazingly, Belcher is already there, sitting beside the Chief and Boska, and several other curious badgers.

'Where've you been?' he says, very pleased with himself. 'Having a picnic?' He doesn't wait to hear what we have to say about that, but carries on. 'You'll never guess where I've been.' He sits waiting for us to take part in his feeble, little quiz, but we don't. 'I've been to the bottom of Lyncombe Hill.' There is a deathly hush. We all know what's down there.

'Did you have a nice stroll, Belcher?' I say, breaking the silence. 'Or did you have some other means of transport, by any chance? Like inside a bucket, maybe?'

He ignores me. 'I finally came up by some steps, where Lyncombe Hill meets Bottom Edge. Followed my nose. But! Guess what I saw. I saw the river. And I saw the bridge.' A great intake of breath goes round the circle of badgers. '*The* bridge. The Halfpenny Bridge. Yes. And beyond that – the Black Tunnel of Death.' Belcher loves to have everybody's attention. He swaggers around. Flora's two have stopped wrestling for once and are sitting perfectly still with their mouths hanging open. 'Oh, yes,' he says. 'Wasn't scared though.' I know I have a story that could match his, but I keep quiet about it.

'Look what he's got,' says the Chief. 'A whole bag of papers.'

'What about the banging and the loops and rainbows of fire over the park?' I ask the Chief. 'Do you reckon that's what Jyk came to warn us about?'

'Could be, Lemmy. Could well be. I haven't studied all this evidence yet. We'll see.'

The Big Match

The next evening, as the last rays of the sun are being snuffed out, all the adult badgers of Beechen Cliff meet in the wide open area in front of the Chief's sett. They've come from opposite ends of the woods.

There's a great feeling of relief. Officially, the committee were the only badgers to know about the coming of Jyk the Treebender, but somehow or other, word, like leaves fluttering in the wind, got around. There are four main networks of chambers with about fifteen badgers in each, so that's a lot of badgers.

The Chief and Boska look pretty smiley as well. Looks like we've nothing to worry about. Time to celebrate. The Chief has a lot of Belcher's papers spread out in front of him.

'What do you make of this, Lemm?'

Picture after picture has two or three humans. They're flying. Lying on the ground. Banging their heads together. Sometimes they appear to have all their arms and legs in a knot. Some pictures show them nuzzling each other. Most of the time, their feet are in the air.

I'm scratching my head on this one, when Mag17 arrives and walks all over the line of papers, from one end to the other, occasionally pecking holes in them. Which is really annoying.

'Baja, baja, twerble, twerble, baja!' Thankfully, this doesn't go on for too long before she flies off.

The Chief says, 'You're a smart young badger,

Lemmy. Apart from the acrobatics, there's something in all of these pictures. You don't get it in other pictures. Can you see what it is?'

It takes me a minute. Then I see what he's talking about. All the sizers are looking at a round thing, or its just leaving their foot or head, or resting on the ground, or being held tightly by one of them. 'What is that, Chief?'

'I've seen them.' Snubber's poking his nose in as usual. 'Seen them on the sweaty field. The half-sizers run around with them. It's a game, like wrestling only with a round thing.'

'What is it?' I ask. 'It's like an enormous oak apple or a filbert.'

'No idea. All I know is it seems to make them go bonkering daft.'

'Hmm,' says the Chief. 'Maybe that's just the thing we need. After all this worry and a night of hiding in our setts with the sky going to blazes. Yup. A bit of daftness.'

I'm about to point out that we don't have an enormous filbert, and, even if we did, we wouldn't be able to see it in the dark, even if we knew how to play this game, which we don't, when I'm hit on the head by an enormous filbert. Except it's nothing like a filbert. It shines. It's a dazzler. And, judging by the fact that it's just come from Mag17 perched on the branch above me, it's obviously one of the bright, shiny things that she loves to collect. 'Twerble! Twerble!' she squawks, as if we knew what she was banging on about.

'Ok, it's a twerble,' I shout up at her, feeling annoyed. But I have to say there is something amazing about it. It bounces off everything it touches. And when it does, it lights up, like a glow-worm.

Immediately, one of Flora's twins, Wendi I think, catches it in her mouth and is pounced on by her brother, Ryn. He wrenches it from her, but is rolled over by Snubber. He picks up the twerble and makes a dash for his sett at the far end of the Cliff, only to be shouldered aside by one of the Bottom Edge badgers. She tries to grab it, but it's bouncing off trees and rocks and seems to be heading for Holloway all by itself. Then it ricochets off the wall this side of Holloway and Bogart pounces on it. He scrapes it backwards with his hind paw. It's madness. The Beechen Cliff badgers have gone as crackers as humans, rolling around, falling over each other and crashing into bushes.

Bogart's back pass has some power behind it and it whizzes past Catlyn's shoulder, thumping the Chief squarely between the eyes. He topples backwards.

Oh, oh!

We all stop where we're standing, though not everyone is standing. Some are upside down in a bramble patch, others are hanging from the lower branches of trees, and others are part of a squirming badger pile.

Boska sniffs around the Chief's face. No sign of breathing. She has a worried look on her face. After a while, she nods and turns sadly towards us. 'This is the way he would have wanted it. Badgers having fun. No fears. No anxieties. Hit between the eyes by a twerble.'

'He was good for us,' says Bogart. Catlyn and me, we let out a sigh.

Then there's a twitch. A snuffling round the nose area. The Chief sits up and says, 'What's the score?'

The game continues. Us Holloway-end badgers have the advantage of Wendi and Ryn who make a great team on their own. They've improvised a routine, passing the twerble to each other just as one of them is about to be blocked by the other side. They're not going straight for our sett. They're up and down banks, underneath ledges, through hollows in some of the dead oaks. When Ryn climbs up part of the Cliff, chased by three of the stronger Bottom Edge lot, he lets the twerble bounce down off stones and tree trunks. With my bad leg, I'm too slow to catch it. But it bounces off Bogart's head, into the path of Catlyn. She cuffs it toward our sett. Senga bars the way of an approaching opponent and Flora flicks it down the hole. Game to us, I believe.

There are a lot of happy badgers around. Everybody, in fact. Except one. The Chief. And it's not on account of the bump on his head. He's staring down, horrified at another picture he's found among the papers. When I reach him, I can see what's bothering him. It's something the whole of Beechen Cliff is about to know about. Not just a few members of the committee.

The picture has three or four badgers lying on the ground. Two of the enemy are standing nearby with long sticks tucked under their arms. One of the humans has his foot on another pile of badgers. They have to be dead badgers, because no badger would just lie there without putting up a fight or making a break for it. Everybody gathers round.

'What does it mean?' says one of the frisky, younger Bottom Edge badgers known as Sonny.

'I don't know, Sonny,' says the Chief, who usually has an answer for most questions.

'It's not good, is it, Chief?' says Sonny.

'No, it's not.'

Mag 17 flutters down. This time she's got a jackdaw with her. Yet another member of the my-brain-is-smaller-than-an-acorn family. It peers at the picture with one beady eye at a time and starts to get into some kind of frenzy. No surprise really. I'm now downgrading my idea of the size of its brain to something like a small raspberry. Anyway, the frenzy continues. 'Baja, baja!' it screeches. 'Baja gull, baja gull!'

'Baja gull,' says Belcher, screwing up his face. 'What's *gull*? Isn't that another of those bird-brains that come up the river, flapping and screaming?'

'It's not *gull*.' The voice is one we've never heard before. It's a deep growl, like a winter wind moaning down in the chambers of our sett. It's as if it comes from far down inside the belly of the Earth. We all turn to see a whopping big bruiser of a badger. Bigger than Bogart. A stranger. Mean-looking, with massive claws like heavy flints and a dangerous scowl around the eyes. He should be hesitant about coming into unknown badger territory, but, as calm as you like, he starts to mark the tree next to him with his scent. That's too much for Belcher who immediately goes for his neck. But, although the stranger is in poor shape, he still manages to sweep Belcher aside. Bogart and I square up to him, standing our ground.

The incomer carries on, undaunted. 'It's not *gull*,' he says again. 'It's *cull*.' He glances round at us all and moves closer. Bogart takes a step towards him and I join him, shoulder to shoulder. The hair on my back is up and I'm ready to attack. This close, I can see that one of his ears is missing. He has scars across his sides. 'Don't you understand what a cull is? The humans. They're planning to wipe you out. Wipe us all out.' When he doesn't get any reaction, he shakes his head. 'You don't get it, do you? They're going to hunt us down. No more Somerset badgers.'

He takes another step forward. 'That's far enough,' I say, barring his way.

'Back off, lads,' says the Chief, and, although both Bogart and I are reluctant, we step aside. He pushes his way between us. I can't tell if he's as casual as he looks or if it's weariness and despair that's taken hold of him.

'Am I right in thinking you're the boss around here?' He looks the Chief up and down.

'What are you doing here? How'd you get in that mess? Who are you? Strolling in here like you own the place?' Belcher is only just getting to his feet and brushing himself off. I glance at Catlyn who looks as if she's ready to pounce if there's any sign that the Chief is in danger. Boska is right beside him too. Her upper lip curls.

'Guns and barbed wire.'

'Guns?' I've never heard the word. I don't think anyone else has either.

The intruder points at the picture lying amongst the dead leaves at the Chief's feet. 'Those sticks in the picture. They're not sticks or twigs or branches as you know them. They're called guns. They sting and they burn. They use them to kill badgers.' Mag17 and her jackdaw friend are flapping up and down as if they know what he's talking about. 'It's how I lost this ear.' He imitated one of the enemy pointing a gun at me and barked loudly and unexpectedly. I tried not to jump. Then with his paw, he drew a straight line through the air towards my head until he touched me between the eyes. I didn't like the smell of him up close. But I didn't look away. Stared him out. He could see I wasn't to be easily frightened. He grunted a mocking laugh, but, as he turned back to the Chief, he seemed to lurch to the side, unbalanced.

'The name's Lombardo. South of Englishcombe. You won't have heard of it. Nice place, but too many cows. One day they just herded them in.

And they don't like badgers near their cows. And the barbed wire? It was the only way I could escape. I had to crawl through a lot of it to get here.'

'We'll be all right,' says Belcher. 'No cows on Beechen Cliff. Besides, we have protection – the Mighty...'

'Button it, Belch,' snaps the Chief. 'That's for us to know.'

'No cows? Huh! That won't stop them. At least, it won't stop *him*. There's one human. Madman. Won't be happy till he's gunned down the last badger in the country. They call him Gagswiller. And he has two hounds. One vicious little thing for ferreting around badger setts and another giant brute who stands waiting at the exit.'

Lombardo's head starts to bow, his legs buckle and he drags himself towards a pile of autumn leaves beyond a tangle of brambles. 'Need rest.'

'We'll think about this, Lombardo,' says the Chief.

'You do that,' is all he manages to mumble over his shoulder and disappears into the darkness.

Sticking to Plan A

'Is this what you call a committee meeting?' complains Snubber. 'These aren't committee members. Senga! You're not part of this.'

'You try and stop me, Snubber. This affects all of us.' We're surrounded by grunts of agreement.

Everybody feels the same as Senga. She's not some badger to argue with. She looks to the Chief for support, but he's in deep thought. He scrapes the earth as if he's drawing patterns in it. He stretches and sinks down. He closes his eyes. A minute passes and we exchange glances, wondering if he's fallen asleep.

Suddenly, he says, 'Number one: we do whatever it takes to get Lombardo back on his feet.'

'What!' exclaim Bogart and Belcher together.

'He walks in here, as calm as you like and...' adds Snubber.

'We nurse him back to health. Feed him up. Build up his strength. You, Senga, and Catlyn, you'll be in charge of that. Should only take a few days.'

'Now wait a minute,' says Catlyn. 'I'm not feeding that great lump.'

'Number two,' says the Chief, ignoring her, 'we can then find out a bit more about what's going on. We need to know what he knows. And number three: whatever he tells us, we need to check it out for ourselves. A scouting party. See the lie of the land. See if what Lombardo says is true.'

'Chief,' I say. Nobody hears me at first because they're all jabbering away to each other. 'Chief!' I say again. 'There's something that bothers me.'

'You're not the only one, Lemm,' Snubber chips in. 'There's a lot that bothers me too.'

'What Lombardo says seems to fit in with the picture Belcher found. The guns and the badgers...lying there.... His advice might save us. But... and I'm not saying this because I can't stand the sight of him... but, what if, on the other hand, his scent brings the dogs straight to us? What if they follow him right here? What if they're on their way right this minute?' There's a hush. 'Don't want to panic anybody or anything.'

'So what you're saying, Lemmy,' says Senga, 'is that Catlyn and me, we could be feeding up this guy for nothing.' I look at Senga and then I look at Catlyn. Catlyn looks at me. I look at the Chief. The Chief looks at me. Senga looks at the Chief. Senga looks at me.

After a moment's pause, the Chief clears his throat and says, 'Thanks, Lemm. We'll be sticking to Plan A.'

In the meantime, Lombardo installs himself in

an old, abandoned sett near the footpath and steps that link Holloway with the clifftop. The network of tunnels and corridors, if you know your way around, eventually join up with our sett. But he's far enough away not to get on anybody's nerves.

For several nights, Catlyn and Senga take him the following: elderberries, worms, shrews, tulip bulbs from a garden in Lyncombe Hill, crab apples, celeriac from the allotments, a lovely ink cap mushroom which I liked the look of myself, a few grubs from under some beech bark, a small lizard – no idea where they found that this time of year – a handful of filberts and acorns, two or three millipedes, and goodness knows what else.

'That's it!' says Senga. It could be blood all over her head and shoulders, but it turns out to be beetroot juice. 'I've had it. He never stops eating. He didn't fancy the beetroot and guess what? Threw it straight back at me!'

Catlyn impersonates our guest. 'Oh dear, I don't think I've got the strength to get up and talk about the enemy. Oh, dear, look at me. I think I'm wasting away. You know what I say to that? Rabbits!'

'Language, Catlyn, language,' says Boska.

I've never seen Catlyn so angry. But, of course, she's right. She looks the Chief straight in the eye and says, 'Chief, I've never seen a badger less likely to waste away than that Lombardo. He has a belly the size of a small haystack. There's never been a healthier badger. He could live through a couple of winters without ever having to leave that sett.'

'Chief,' I say, taking Catlyn's side. 'Maybe this Lombardo doesn't know as much as he says he does. Maybe he's just after a free supper.'

'Then what do you suggest, Lemmy?'

'Let me take him his food tomorrow night. I'll figure out something.'

'You're welcome,' says Senga.

Next dusk, I make a special trip, collect a whole load of goodies for Lombardo and, before the sun rises, deliver it to his front door. As morning comes, we all return to our setts to sleep the rest of daylight hours. Little chance of that. A rumble, low and distant, starts to echo along the corridors and passageways of the sett. It gets louder and scarier. It's as if Beechen Cliff is at the centre of an earthquake. It's like giant boots walking above us, or the enemy driving their dozers into the remaining rockpiles of the ruined houses. Thud! Kaboom! Wham! Bam! It's difficult to identify the source of the noise. We're surrounded by reverberations. The underground tremors send a bunch of younger badgers in my direction. Their faces appear out of the gloom of various tunnels, their noses and ears twitching. The Chief and Boska are there too. I have a smile on my face.

'Lemmy,' says Boska, her voice full of suspicion. 'What do you know about this?'

I let them wait, enjoying the moment, as another rumbling bombardment bounces its way down one chamber and ricochets out another.

'I took Lombardo his food as I said. A big heap. A special treat.'

'And…?'

'Jerusalem artichokes.' For a moment there's silence. Then the Chief falls backwards nearly knocking himself unconscious and wetting himself at the same time. Boska wanders off chuckling. The younger badgers say things like, 'Whoa!' and fan their noses. Nobody gets any sleep, but when evening comes, Lombardo appears. Seems to be able to walk perfectly well. He peers at me through half-closed eyes.

'Feeling better now, Lombardo?' I say.

He glowers at me and nods. 'Never mind that. Let's get down to business.'

Bit by bit, he describes what we should be looking for. We send out scouting parties. Bogart, of course, knows his way in and out of the Bear Flat gardens. He takes a few helpers with him. Belcher, Senga, Flora and Snubber scour Lyncombe Hill for clues, and, while they're at it, pass the word on to the Lyncombe Vale badgers. Another group keep an eye on Holloway, though we don't think the attack will come from that direction. Catlyn, Lombardo, Sonny from Bottom Edge and I investigate Greenway Lane for any of the signs that he's mentioned. The smell and sound of more dogs than usual around, being brought in for the hunt. Guns in windows. Boots by the doors. More rattletraps along the roadside, hot and fuming from being driven some distance. And worst of all,

Gagswiller's own special rattletrap – a monstrous thing, with the black, squiggly marks we've seen in the enemy's papers, and... and... a horrific thing: the skin of a dead badger tied to the front.

Fortunately, we don't see any of these things.

These expeditions go on night after night. Then after about a week, on another scouting trip, a rattletrap races along Greenway Lane, squealing and screeching, and hits Sonny. Poor kid! Doesn't have a chance. Bang! Thump! He's gone. We can see him near the grass bank, mangled, not moving. Another step and he would have been safe. Lombardo's the only one who can bear to go near him. Sniffs around, comes back over, says nothing. He stops. He's standing, looking dazed, in the middle of the road. He's staring straight past me into the open door of a rattletrap house. I can't see a thing among the dark shadows, though the smell, a bit like dog but nothing like I've smelt before, is overpowering.

Then, suddenly, there's a blinding light, a roar, the hot smell of another rattletrap. He doesn't hear it. There's no time to think. I should run, but instinctively

I hurl myself at Lombardo. I bowl him over with all my weight as the roar whizzes past us. We lie in a heap, breathless. Lombardo says nothing. Doesn't thank me for saving his life. Nothing. Nothing at all, as we make our way back under the gate, into the field, through the allotments and home.

When we report back, the news about Sonny hits everybody hard, though not as hard as the enemy hit Sonny. Everybody is quiet. But I'm looking at the Chief and I don't like what I see. He looks older than ever, and worse, he looks defeated. He's muttering to himself. 'Poor Sonny.' It seems to take all his strength to turn to the assembled badgers and start his familiar call. 'How do badgers learn?'

'The hard way,' reply one or two sad voices. There's not much enthusiasm for joining in the old response.

'No,' I say. Did I say that? Must have. It's gone eerily quiet. Everybody's staring at me as if I've said something very, very rude beginning with R. I say it again. The word 'No' rings around the banks and ridges of Beechen Cliff. 'We've got to do something. This time, learning the hard way means that, soon, there won't be any badgers left to learn anything. We can't sit around waiting for it to come, whatever it is.' I look at the surrounding faces. They're waiting for me to say more.

'Lemmy's right.' It's Lombardo. 'We didn't see any guns tonight, or extra boots by the door. There weren't the long lines of green rattlebang monsters that surrounded us down Englishcombe way. But I saw something tonight. I've seen them before. Badger-baiters. Terriers. I saw them just after Sonny was killed. Tied up and muzzled. There's no escape from badger-baiters.'

'Are you sure, Lombardo? The badger setts of Beechen Cliff have any number of entrances and exits. They can't cover them all.'

'That's not a problem for the baiters, Lemmy. They'll find you.'

Everybody's looking at the Chief, including Boska, but he has nothing to say. For once, Snubber is silent. The twins aren't wrestling. Catlyn comes and stands close to me.

I start to think on my feet. 'Well... if there's no protection for us here... that means ... we have to be somewhere else... somewhere they won't find us. Or! Somewhere they wouldn't expect to find us. That's it! That's what we do.'

'What do we do, Lemmy?' asks Belcher.

'Tell us, Lemmy,' says Snubber.

'We leave here and move into the enemy gardens.'

'What!' exclaims Snubber. 'Into the sizers' own territory! Joking aren't you?'

'It's the only way. They won't be looking there. And if we spread out into the gardens of Greenway Lane, Bear Flat, Holloway, Bottom Edge and Lyncombe Hill, it will at least give some of us, maybe all of us, a chance.' I check the faces surrounding me. No sign of agreement, doubt, nothing. Just blank.

'One smart badger!' Lombardo pitches in. 'Lemmy's right. It's the only chance we've got. And we have to take it now, before it's too late. One other thing – so far we've seen no sign of Gagswiller. But he's here. I know it. We just haven't sniffed him yet.'

All the badgers of Beechen Cliff gather the following dusk. Word is passed back through the ranks from older ones to young ones, from sisters to brothers, from watchful mates to eager offspring, from Holloway-end badgers to Bottom Edge badgers. I tell them who is to go where. Reassure them the plan will work. Lie low till the baiting is past. We're all ready when the Chief says, 'Good luck. But I won't be coming.'

'Chief?' says Boska. 'Of course, you're coming. Lemmy's chosen a nice garden in Lyncombe Hill for us, haven't you, Lemmy?'

'No, Boska,' he insists. 'You go. It's a great plan of Lemmy's. Brilliant plan. But I'm too old. I'll hide. Nobody knows the chambers like I do. I'll see you all when you come back. I'll be here waiting.'

Suddenly, there's a howl. Several howls. Echoing across the park. There's no time to argue. The muzzles are off.

Breaking through the Enemy Ring

Bogart leads the way, closely followed by Senga. My leg slows me down, but I urge them to carry on. I'll catch them up. We don't have any trouble with the baiters. The main thrust of their advance on Beechen Cliff seems to be up the main field and over Alexandra

Park and the sweaty school field. But Lombardo and Catlyn should be with us. They should certainly be overtaking me at the rate I go. Of course, there are badger-ways everywhere, crisscrossing the Cliff, up on the top and through the surrounding area. Maybe they've passed me taking a side road.

Every time I hear the squeals and barking of the baiters, I wonder if they've found one of our friends from the Cliff. As I've already said, badgers don't say much, don't call out, so I don't know if anyone's been caught or not.

'Where's Catlyn?' Bogart and Senga glance at each other then at me. They're hiding in a thick, leafy corner of a garden on the edge of Bear Flat – one we've been through before.

'We thought she was with you,' says Senga. 'Don't worry, Lemmy. She's smart. She'll be fine.' But she doesn't turn up that night.

The next day, we keep a lookout, one of us at a time. Something is happening inside the humans' house. Sizers are going in and out, in and out non-stop. At dusk the lights come on. A half-sizer is standing leaning over a long black box. Rain is pouring out of her eyes. Eventually the lights go off. The next morning, she is there again, standing beside the box. Soon, some more humans come and take the box away. They carry it high on their shoulders. The half-sizer stands at the window. Rain is still falling from her eyes. Her face is streaked with water lines. It's the half-sizer I saw in the woods, walking together, attached at the hands, with Jyk the Treebender. The same one who cut the strings from Catlyn.

Too scared of being discovered, we haven't moved much from our spot. We've eaten a few worms, but not much else. Two nights have passed without the baying of the dogs.

'We should be going back,' says Bogart. Senga nods but neither of us moves. What will we find?

Something is happening. The wooden door of the stone box house is opening. The half-sizer comes out with a box of carrots, parsnips and meat. When she goes back to standing by the window, we attack the box of food like we've never seen food before. We don't care that she's watching us, clicking her little shiny box.

Once the fat moon hauls itself lazily up above the horizon, it doesn't take long for us to retrace our steps back to the Cliff. It takes longer to get used to what we find.

Lots of entrances to the setts have been trampled and dug up. Small bonfires are still smouldering outside some of them. Badgers are wandering around aimlessly. Some obviously hurt.

'Where's your Mighty Jyk now, Lemmy?' It's Snubber. He looks bedraggled with a wound, a bite, to his shoulder.

'We're alive, Snubber.'

'Not all of us, Lemmy.' It's Flora calling. 'We found the Chief. Over here.'

'No,' I say, even though I had half-expected as much. 'Not the Chief.'

'Put up a fight, I reckon,' she says. 'Looks like he took one of them with him.'

I nod. 'Always was a fighter.' There's a baiter lying dead beside him. Learnt the hard way.

One after another, the badgers return. I examine every face. None of them belongs to Catlyn. I make a sweep of the entire underground maze of the Cliff, every blade of grass of its rough, tumbling surface. Every inch of trodden buttercups and cow parsley has the lingering smell of the assault, dog and human scent on every dandelion leaf, root and rock. Prints in the soft earth, scratches on tree trunks. Here and there, badger fur is caught on bramble and wild rose creeper. Drops of blood on stone and leaf. The place, our wonderful Beechen Cliff, has been a battlefield.

And yet, whenever I enter a sett, I'm welcomed. Badgers I know, and many I don't, say, 'Thanks, Lemmy. You saved us.' Some have lost a brother or sister or both. A parent or grandparent is dead. A baby missing. And sometimes I come across signs of that loss. It's sickening. But still I hear the words of welcome: 'Thanks, Lemmy. You saved us.'

I climb to the top of the Cliff and to the bottom, I tunnel deep, and search from one end to the other until I'm exhausted. No sign of Catlyn anywhere.

It's early morning when I hear some commotion back at the old Chief's sett. Lombardo has returned with a tale. But there's no light of enjoyment in his eye in the telling of it.

'They came over the Cliff before we all got out. Some from the Holloway steps. A lot of us were herded towards Bottom Edge. We thought we'd be fine. That open space where the wall ends, we'd get out there and into the gardens. Somebody said he knew a churchyard we could hide in.'

'Catlyn?' I say.

'She was there when another swarm of humans and their baiters came right at us from Bottom Edge. I counted about eighteen or nineteen, maybe twenty enemy. They had their baiters on long ropes at that stage. Catlyn took us down some chambers and out the other side of them. But someone must have turned. They came after us. We ran and ran. Didn't stop at the churchyard. Got too far into enemy country. Busy roads.'

'So where is she?'

'That's when we saw a line of rattletraps race by, wailing and howling, with their blue lights spinning around on the top. The baiters stopped chasing and we laid low in some shrubs.'

Belcher interrupts. For the first time, I notice that his tail is damaged, matted and raw. He must be in pain. He doesn't complain, but he coughs and splutters as he speaks. 'I saw the rattletraps arrive. The humans in black. They got out. Spoke to the other humans and their baiters. It took a while to stop the attack, but eventually they left.'

I glare at Lombardo. 'What about Catlyn?'

'I don't know how long we stayed there. We were getting hungry. As soon as I poked my nose out, I was spotted and we were chased out into the open. That's when it happened.' He leans on a tree stump and takes a breath.

'What happened?' asks Boska, gently.

'Gagswiller. I saw him coming along the road. Unmistakable. Some of the enemy were laughing and pointing at the badger pelt tied to his monster rattletrap. Others were throwing stones at it and waving papers on sticks. He drove slowly towards us. I could see his face. His shiny teeth. Then he speeded up. We started to run. We got split up. He swerved and came after me, but he crashed into a wall. I couldn't see where Catlyn was to begin with. Then there she was. Almost under his wheels. He was forced to go backwards and she escaped... for the time being.'

'What do you mean,' I say, 'for the time being?' My breathing is short and fast and I can hear my heart beating.

'I could see the two dogs inside the rattletrap and they saw me. We've seen each other before. They were yelping and growling. In a frenzy. They wanted my skin. But Gagswiller roared forward again. Bore down on Catlyn. Crossed roads. Crossed the humans' pathways. Half-sizers had to jump out of his way. But he couldn't reach Catlyn.'

'Then she's safe? She's all right?'

Lombardo's head is down. Slowly, he looks up. Looks me straight in the eye. 'He can't reach Catlyn, Lemmy, because she's running across the Halfpenny Bridge and into the Black Tunnel of...'

He doesn't get a chance to finish. I launch myself at him. Knock him sideways. Bite into his shoulder. Cuff him around the head. But, although he's twice my size, he doesn't fight back. Lies there and takes it. I want to kill him. And he might have let me kill him, if there were no badgers around to pull me off him. Boska's there. Belcher and Senga.

'No,' I wail, curling up among the buttercups and cow parsley. 'Not Catlyn. Not her.'

Lombardo has struggled to his feet. He's there beside me too. 'I'm sorry, Lemmy. I'm so sorry.'

Gagswiller

I wander the Cliff. Night after night and even during some daylight hours. Crazy, I know. But the danger has passed, or maybe I don't care. The place looks different in daytime. I avoid badgers wherever I can. Life is slowly returning to normal – for most of us anyway. It'll soon be light now. It's getting colder.

Maybe it'll snow soon. Maybe I'll head back and go underground. Maybe there's no point to any of it.

'You talking to yourself again, Lemm?' It's Belcher. Wandering back from the allotments. Seems to be feeling a bit more like his old self again. Still got a cough though. Drags his tail.

'Yep, Belch,' I answer wearily. 'Talking to myself. Thinking about things.'

'That's your problem, Lemm. Think too much.'

'True. How's your tail?'

'It'll do. But as far as thinking is concerned, maybe you need to think about this.' He lays a carrot under my nose and steps back. 'We'll be needing a new Chief.'

'So?'

He doesn't say anything. Gives a little sharp nod of the head, and strolls off, chuckling and wheezing. As he disappears down the nearest tunnel, he peers over his shoulder and says, 'Think about it.'

I don't think about it. I carry on.

Something draws me to Bottom Edge. I hear a noise. I smell the enemy. Of course, their houses are close by there, but this is something else. I drop down into a ditch under some rhododendrons. A half-sizer is exploring the thicker parts of the wood. She takes a few steps and stops. Takes a few more, stops and gazes carefully around her. Always silent. No talking into a box. I can't see her face. I have nothing to lose now, so I follow her – not usual badger behaviour, I know. I shudder when I realise this is more like dog behaviour, but I continue.

There's something about her that makes me curious. Then I see why. She has a knife and a rope. She stands in front of one of the setts. One that has been dug wide open by the baiters. That's when I see her face. Its moon white with two black stripes from her eyes down to her chin. I've never seen an enemy half-sizer looking like that before.

Surprised, I break a twig and crunch a crisp rhododendron leaf. She doesn't move, but her eyes flash in my direction. Normally, that's the signal for making a dash for it, but I don't. She doesn't come any closer. Instead, at the speed of a snail, she kneels down and places a piece of crumpled paper on the ground beside her. She opens it and inside are a pile of worms, wriggling, with that unmistakable earthy smell. I stay put. She doesn't move. She is still kneeling beside the worms as I cautiously creep out of hiding. A few steps away from her, I hesitate. The temptation is too great. In a rush, I scurry towards the feast, eat them all and run back to safety. When I look back, she's leaving as silently as she came.

I have met the new Jyk.

The following evening, when only bats, owls, mice, foxes and badgers are out and about, every daytime creature is woken abruptly. Startled by drumming, throbbing, grinding machinery that sounds like cleavers splitting the air. A horn blares non-stop. A cackling human voice and the howls of dogs. A rattletrap has driven off the road onto the open bank at Bottom Edge.

Every badger on Beechen Cliff comes running in my direction.

'What do we do, Chief?' says Senga. I wonder what she's talking about.

'She's talking to you, Lemmy,' says Lombardo.

She repeats the words – heavy, desperate, pleading words. 'What do we do?'

'Climb up to the setts on the highest part of the Cliff. And if you get a sniff of the dogs closing in, spread out and run to the gardens.'

'What about you, Chief?'

'Go!' I say. 'Go now!' The frosted floor of the woods appears to sway and shimmer as waves of badgers head off up the slopes and rocky outcrops of the Cliff. 'You too, Lombardo.'

'You know who it is, don't you, Lemmy?'

'I can guess.'

'What's your plan?'

'Don't have one.'

He gazes down at me and gives me a gentle cuff round the head, the way young wrestling badgers do. He stretches up to his full height. 'What are we waiting for?'

We soon spot him tramping towards us, still some way off, crunching the frosted leaves and cursing the tripping roots and uneven ground. So that's a gun, I think.

'That's a gun,' whispers Lombardo, reading my

thoughts. He shakes his head and says, 'He won't beat you with it. He can stand at Bottom Edge and kill you at Holloway-end. Watch out for the tiny red spot of light on your fur. It'll turn to blood before you hear the crack of the gunshot.'

The gun is tied to his shoulder. In his other hand, a white light flashes in all directions. The yellow streetlamps of Holloway shine on his sharp-stone face. He has a nose like a buzzard's beak, popping rabbit eyes, and long, sneering teeth. His back and arms are covered in grey badger pelts. Two dogs are at his side. A light breeze brings his scent in our direction. His smell is sickening, but I wanted to see him.

Although I have no real plan, one thing I aim to do is keep him away from our badgers for as long as possible. We dive down a nearby sett. We can get behind him through our underground tunnels. Did we make too much noise? Maybe. For the little unruly baiter dog follows, yelping its stupid head off. Seems a bit hyper to me. I wonder what Gagswiller feeds it on? We're not too worried about it. It's the other dog, the enormous hound-monster, that comes up to the hunter's waist, that scares me.

It feels safer in our own world below the surface. I know these tunnels so well. I grew up in them. Dug some of them. Lombardo, on the other hand, is a bit on the chunky side and can't get through them all without a bit more excavating. As he scrapes away earth, I pile it up behind us, blocking up corridors as we go. That'll slow the baiter down, I think. There are so many wrong paths down here. The little yelper should be confused in the pitch dark. We have a head start.

We emerge, well behind Gagswiller, close to a stone house, ruined a long time ago, in the old Chief's great, great, great grandfather's day. All the while, I'm thinking we haven't seen the hound-monster yet. With my leg slowing me a bit, Lombardo is ahead of me when the baiter, that twitchy Mr. Yelper, appears from nowhere. How did it do that? Must have got lucky. The noise it makes starts off Gagswiller. 'Gerra gerra, radik, baja, baja!'

The nasty baiter picks me off, jumps on my back and rolls me over. It has a grip of my fur, some skin too, but I lash out at it and it backs off. Gagswiller screeches and the baiter leaps at me again. We're locked together. My teeth are clamped around a leg. There is a cry from Lombardo who's racing to help me. 'Red spot, Lemmy! The light!' He's right. There it is, over my heart. I use all my strength to try to free myself. I twist around. There is a sudden loud crack and the baiter falls dead. I don't hang about.

As we reach a hole in the crumbling wall of the house, the red light is fluttering all around us - on the ground at our feet, hovering on the ruined building ahead of us. There is a gunshot. It takes a chunk out of the stone. A second knocks some leafless branch from a sycamore. Another, and Lombardo slumps to the ground. Gagswiller is getting closer as I haul Lombardo by the scruff of the neck in through the wall. But he's heavy and I collapse over him as soon as we're inside.

I've never been in this place before. This ancient human house. It's open to the sky. The breeze whistles through the cracks in the fragile walls. There is an open space on the far side where humans would have moved in and out. Over the years, some birch and ash have pushed their way up through the floor of fallen stone covered in moss. I see all this in a few breaths - my breaths, that is, for I don't know if Lombardo has many left. Staying here is out of the question.

Then, above my head, there is a low, sinister growl. It comes from the bottomless chasm that is the vile throat of the hound-monster. Its hellish eyes pore over me from its chosen position on the top of a wall, sizing me up and down as if I'm not worth the puny effort it will take to kill this weary, limping badger. It's so big, it leaps down into the building effortlessly. Taking its time, it moves its grotesque head this way and that. It sniffs at Lombardo. Shoves his body out of the way with a flick of its heel. In its own good time, it draws closer. As I back myself into a corner, the sight of it terrifies me. Leering, dead eyes. Claw-marks across its face from previous fights. The smell of its drooling mouth disgusts me. I feel the cold stone at my back. I can go no further. I'm going to die here in this place, where I stand. But not without a fight. Not without inflicting as much damage and pain as I can on this savage brute.

For a second, it turns away. But I know this is it.

A trick. I don't wait. I go for the throat. It hurls me to one side. It stands over me. Its eyes say, 'Last prayer to Jyk, badger.' That's when Lombardo hits him from the side. His full weight against the beast's shoulder. They tussle, rolling across the floor. Lombardo's swiped to one side, winded when he hits the wall. But as the creature leaps at him, Lombardo's jaws lock around its throat. Their struggle shakes loose some of the balancing stones of the wall. There's blood, but most of it belongs to the hound. They crash against the wall again. With a casual flick of the great animal's head, Lombardo is thrown at my feet, but the monster is weakened. It ignores the stone that thumps onto the ground beside it. But it can't ignore the rest of it. The wall collapses on top of it. An avalanche of house-rock rumbles and cracks. That's it. The beast won't move again.

'Lombardo,' I say. His eyes are open. 'You killed it.'

He stares in the direction of my voice, but he can't really see me. 'I owed you one, Lemm.' He tries to say more, but nothing comes out. I sit with him as he fades away, his story sinking deep into the dark earth of Beechen Cliff.

I'm still leaning over Lombardo when I'm caught in a circle of white light. The circle moves across the rock-strewn floor to the pile that has entombed Gagswiller's hound. 'Radda mocho baja baja staka ridda baja!' His fury thunders through the trees of the Cliff, across Holloway and the Bottom Edge. All the badgers of Beechen Cliff hear it. The enemy across the valley must hear it.

Gagswiller points his light back again at where Lombardo lies. I'm no longer there. I'm shuffling as fast as I can through the doorway at the other side of the house. I've seen something. A human face. It's white as the moon with two black stripes running from the eyes to the chin.

'Baja,' whispers Jyk softly. She points to the ground behind her. Gagswiller stomps towards us, shouting. He raises his gun. When the red beam passes her and touches my head, she leans to the side and catches it in the palm of her hand. When the red light moves, she moves too. This makes our predator roar in frustration. As he moves closer, she moves deeper into a thicker swathe of undergrowth. She holds out her hand to Gagswiller and curls her fingers. It makes him follow.

The ground is rough here, but Jyk is surefooted. Gagswiller curses as he puts a foot down a hole, stumbles over rocks and gets entangled in arching brambles, but still he pushes through. Then I realise Jyk has stopped. Though I'm behind her, I'm anxious that we've reached a clearing in a circle of young birch trees. Nowhere to hide. Gagswiller takes a step closer, raising his gun. But his foot is caught in a tough raspberry root or a winding rose. He tugs at it angrily. Tugs again. 'Gegga racha warra rowa gragragra!' He fires.

I don't know where the shot has gone, but it doesn't hit me or Jyk. A tree is unbending. His foot is rising in the air. His gun goes off again. He screams and fires again and again, as the rope lifts his body off the ground and he dangles helplessly in the air. I've never seen a big-sizer upside down before.

I can hear wailing rattletraps getting closer as I sit beneath him looking up at his popping rabbity eyes.

Somehow, my presence makes him wave and shake his arms even more. Doesn't do him any good. The gun falls from his hands. There's a crackle of cold leaves behind me and Jyk the Treebender has gone. I creep back into the shadows when the humans in black arrive. They pick up his gun. They don't take long to cut him down. They talk to him when he's on his feet again. When he tries to run away, they grab him by the arms and remove him hollering from Beechen Cliff.

Staggering back to my sett, I meet Senga, who has bravely ventured out to help. 'Spread the word,' I say. 'Tell them it's over.'

I don't know how long I sleep. When I stick my nose out, the world is black and white. Badger-coloured. Two young badgers are wrestling, tumbling over each other. In the middle of their game, they say things like, 'And Lombardo did this, then Lemmy the Chief did that.' Footprints in the snow tell me a magpie has been here looking for me. Belcher is muttering to himself about a piece of rope he's found.

'You talking to yourself, Belch?' I say. He snorts and, chuckling, he nods his head.

I step outside and smell the cold, muffled air.

Winter is here on Beechen Cliff.

Spring will surely come.

Printed in Great Britain
by Amazon.co.uk, Ltd.,
Marston Gate.